a Party

SHREWBETTINA'S BIRTHDAY

John S. Goodall

Harcourt Brace Jovanovich, Inc., New York
Copyright © 1970 by John S. Goodall. All rights reserved.
ISBN 0-15-274080-5. Printed in Japan.
First American editon, 1971.

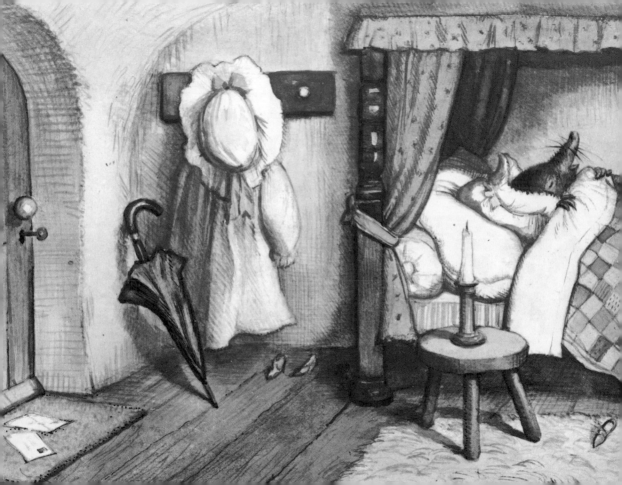

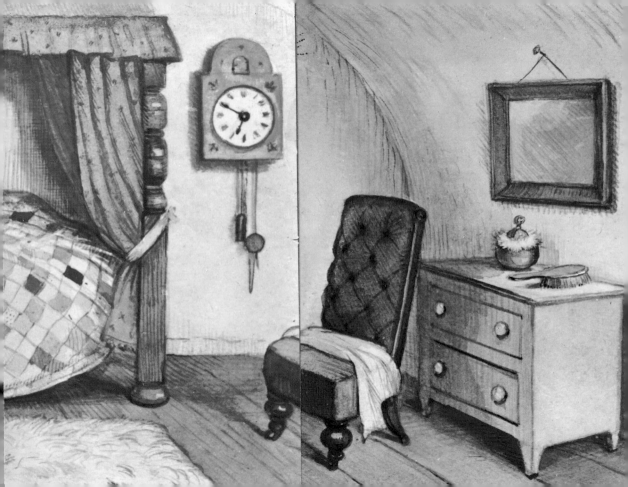

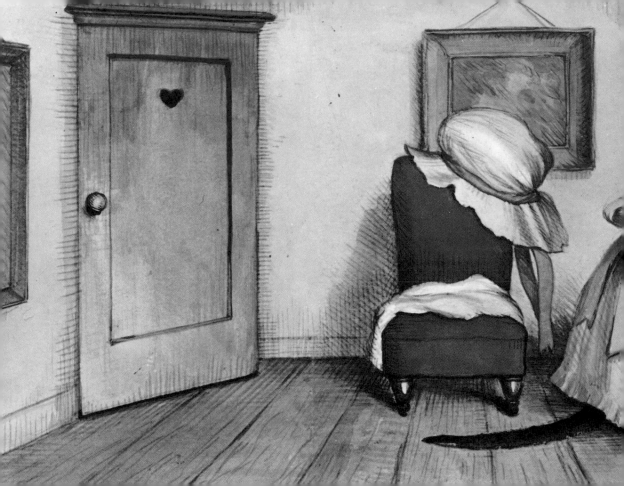

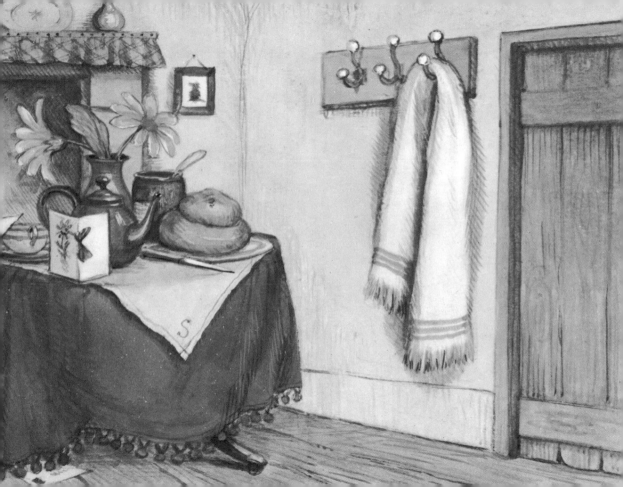

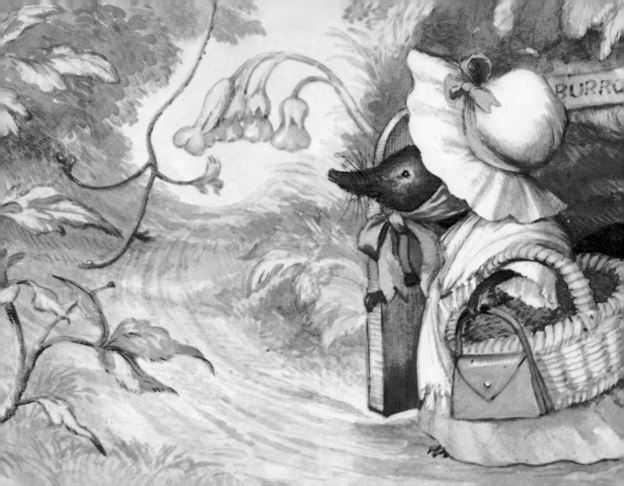

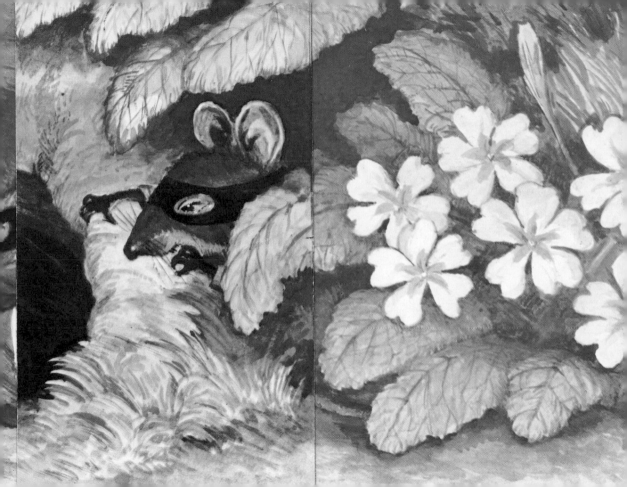

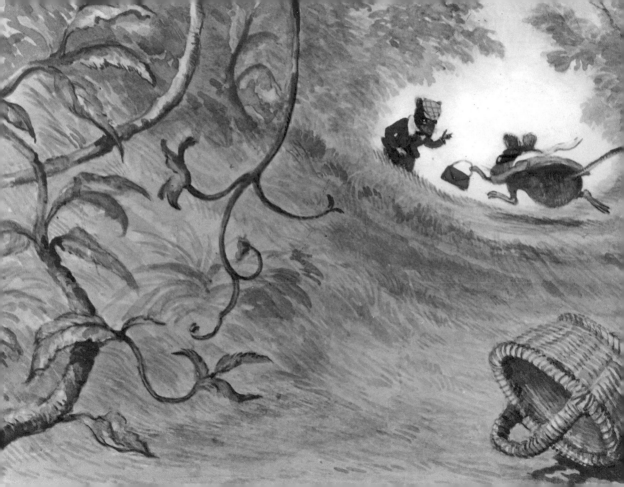

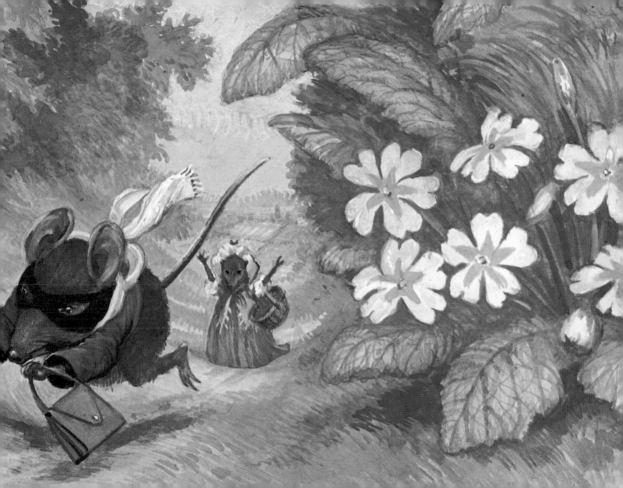

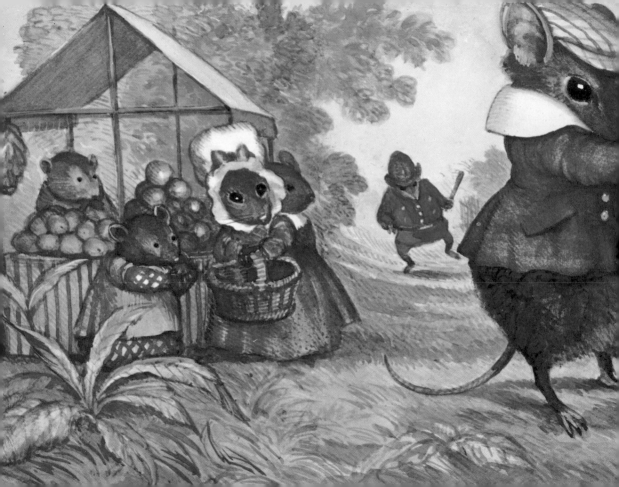

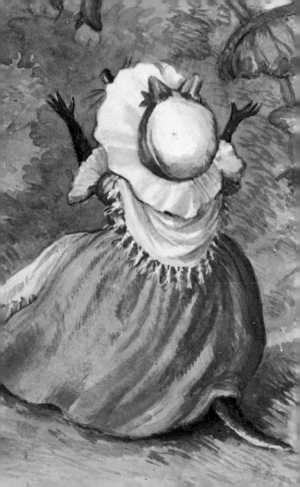

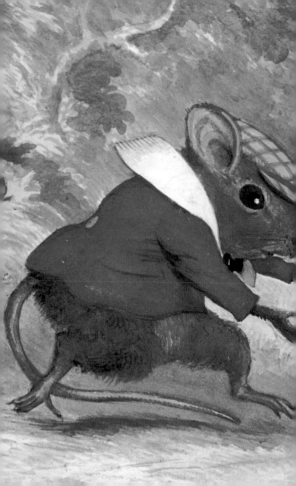

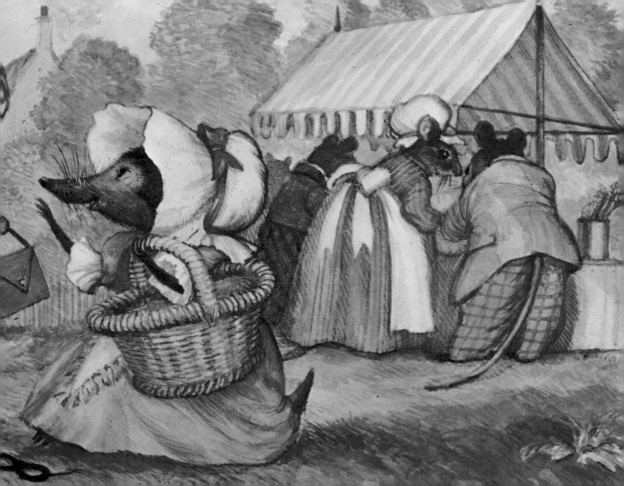

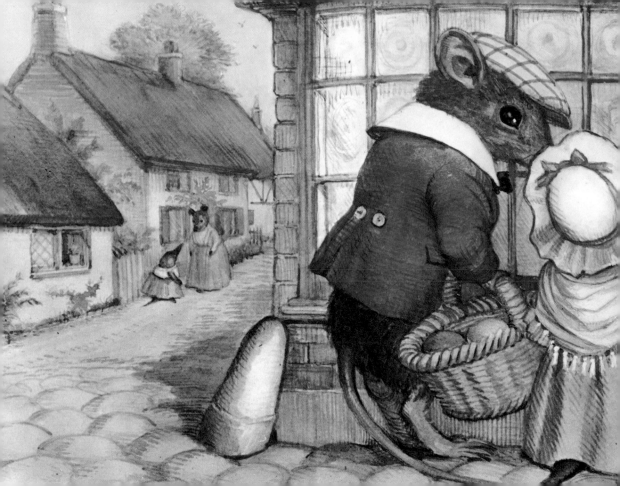

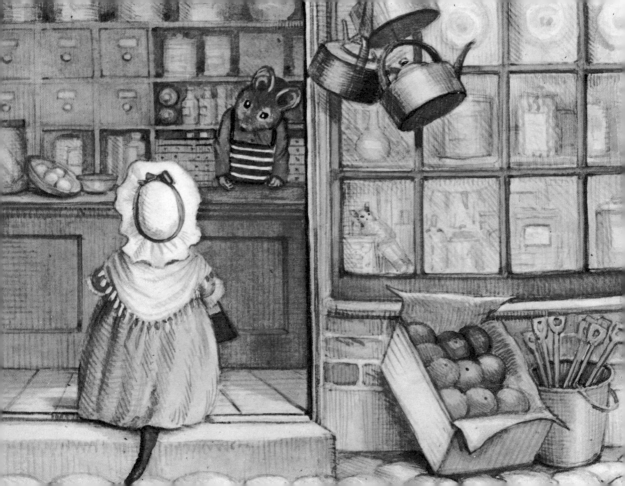

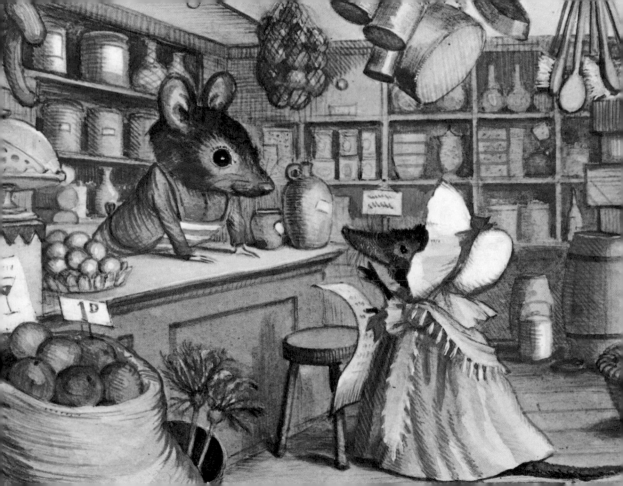

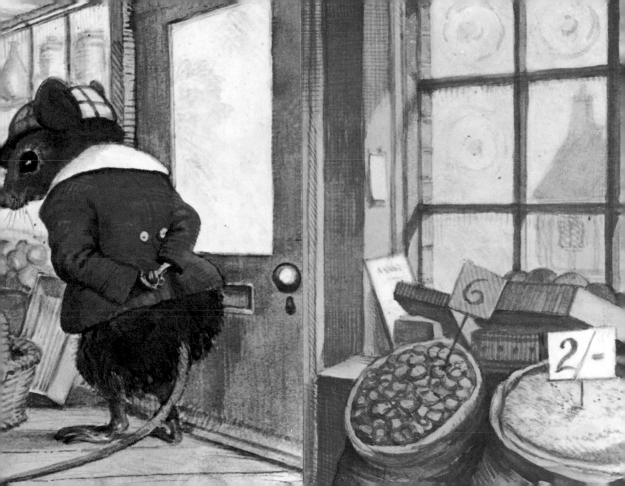

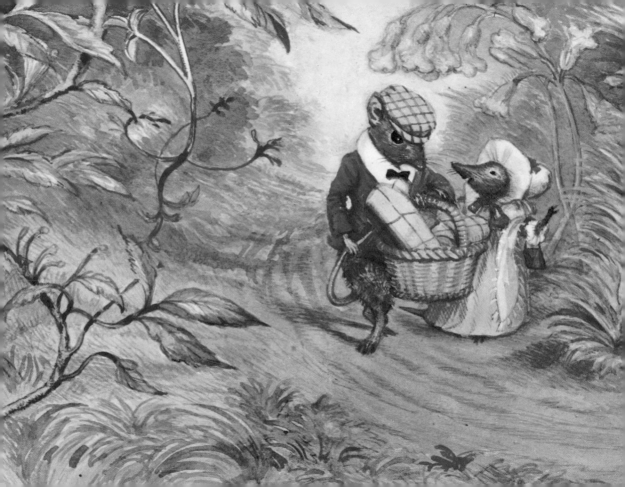

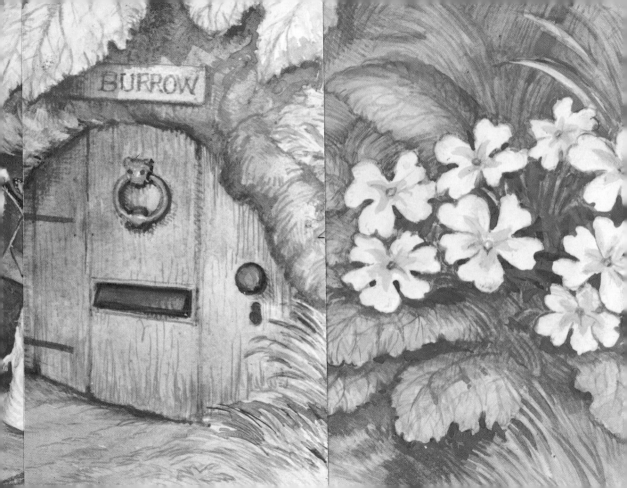

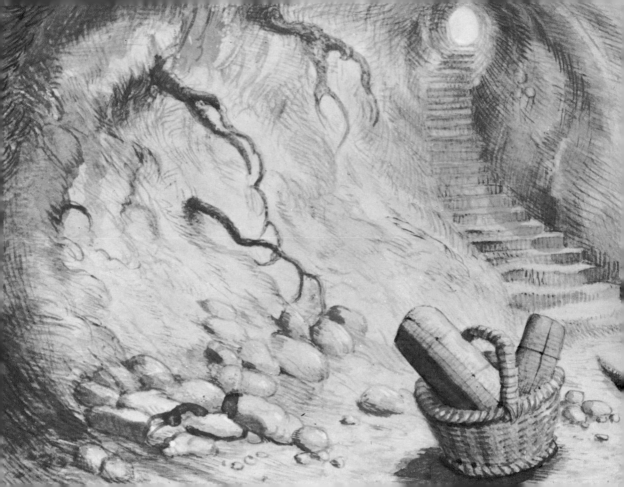

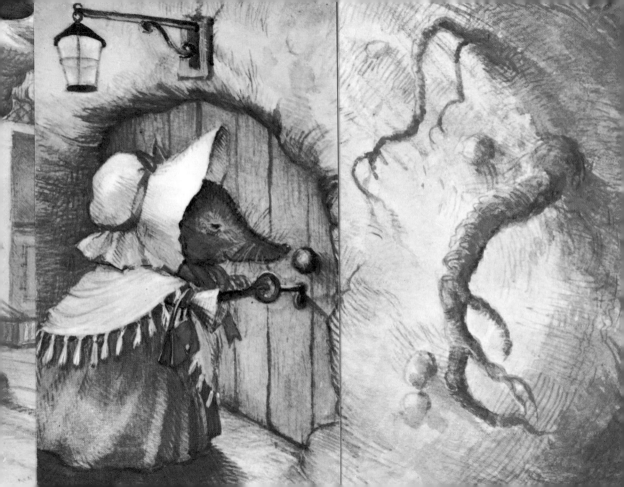

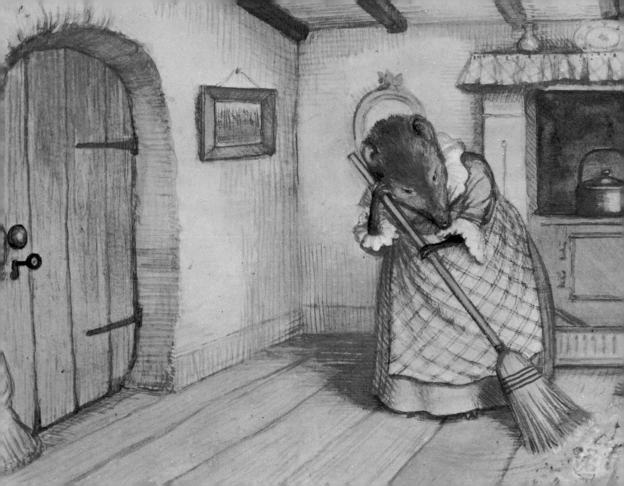

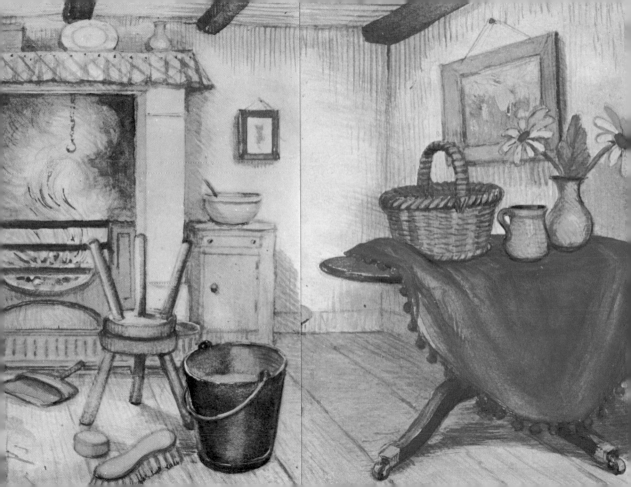

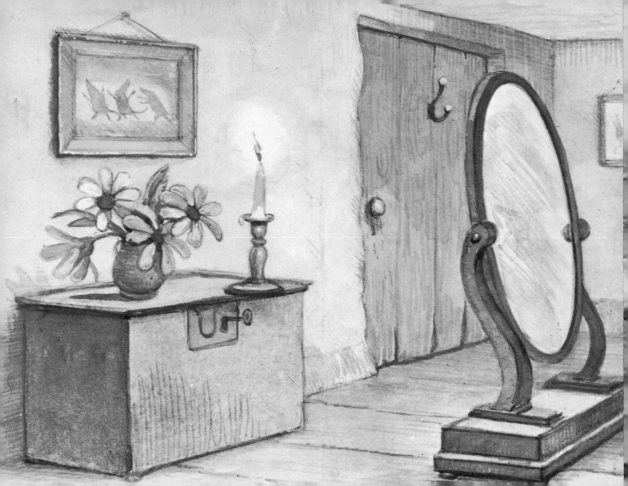

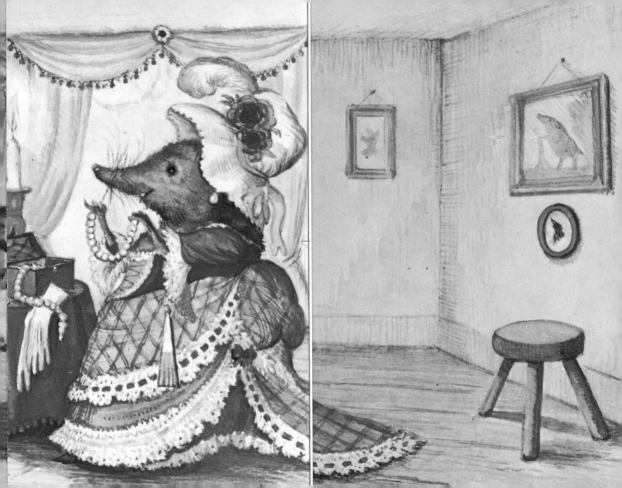

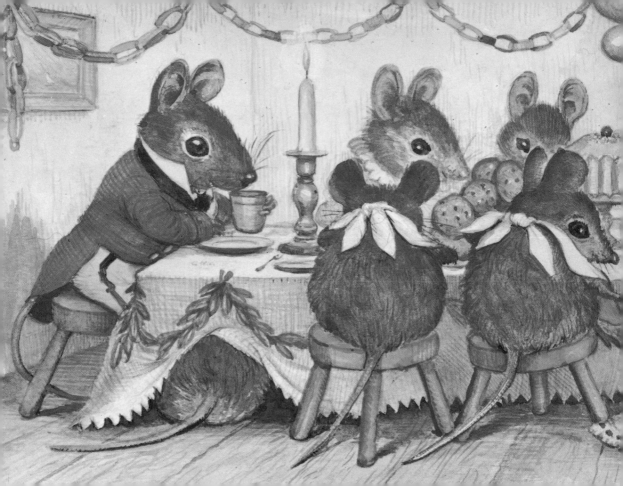

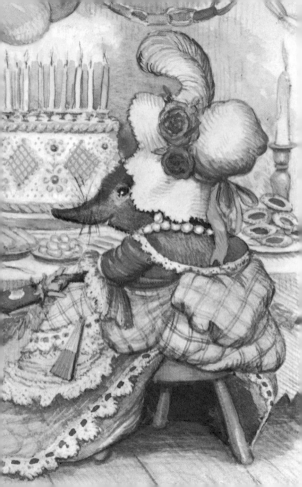

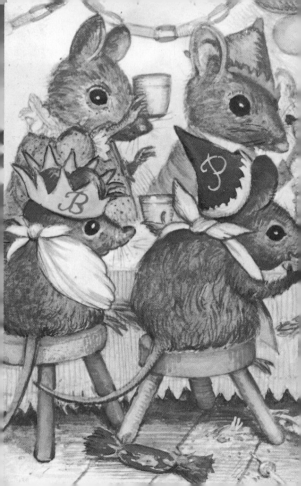

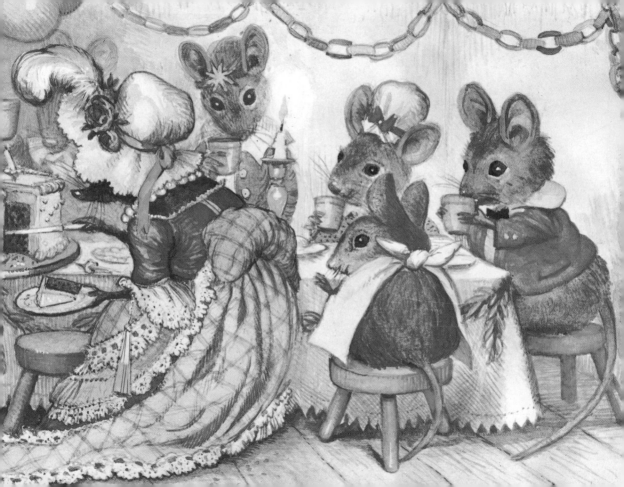

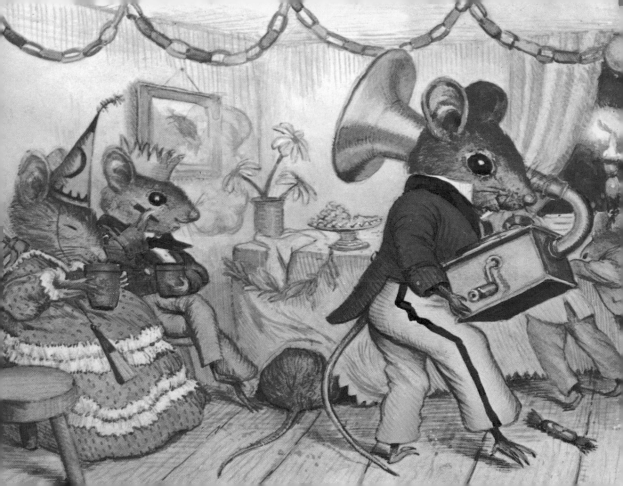

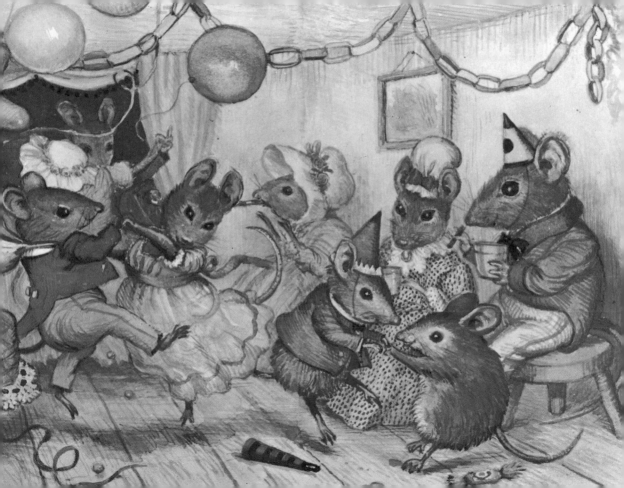

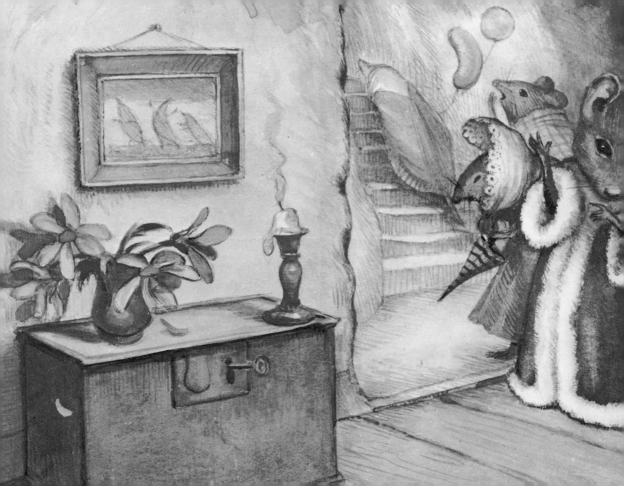

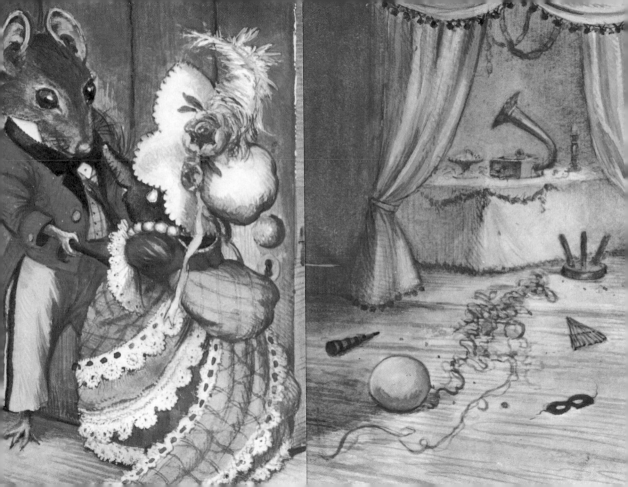

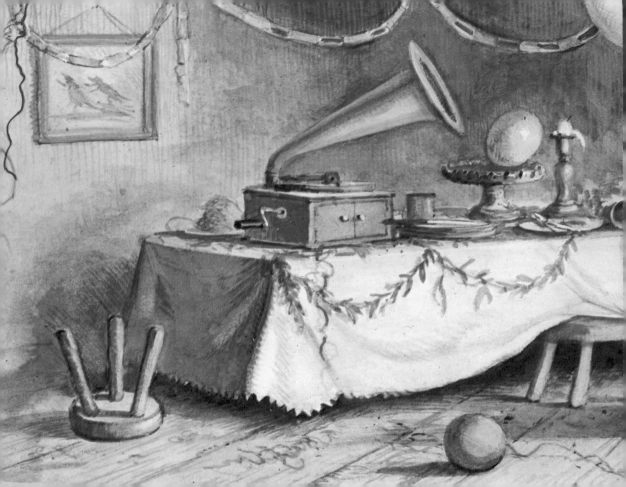

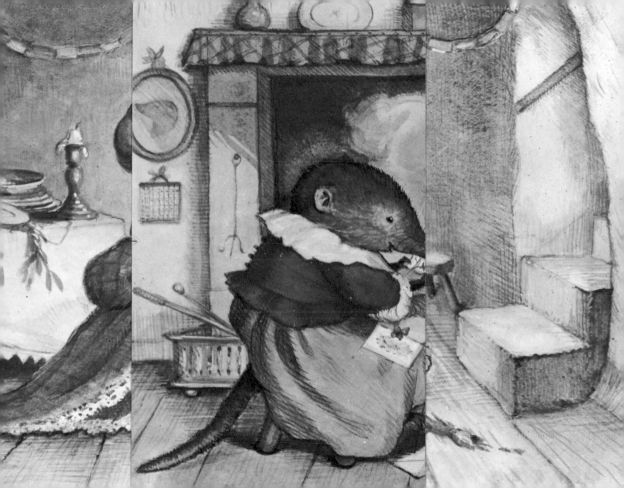

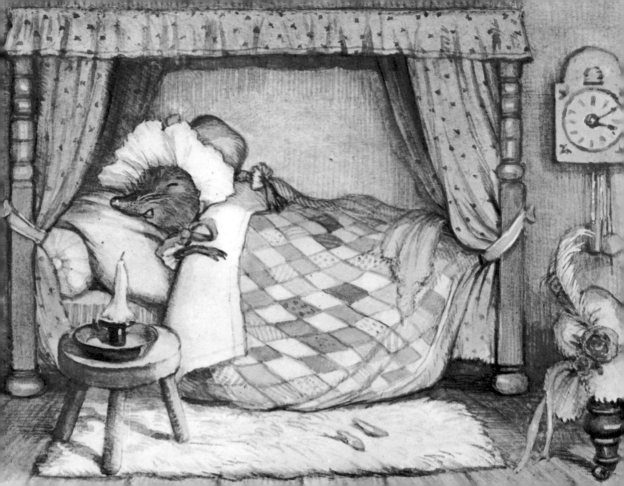

Good